D1597068

TICK REX
QUEEN OF THE WOODS

For Melinda, David, Ethan, and Brandon
Stay out of the woods!

To the lion, stay cowardly
— Tick Rex

Tick Rex: Queen of the Woods

Copyright © 2023 by Ruth Thomas
Cover and internal illustrations © 2023 by Russell A. Thomas

Publisher: Peck-A-Long Publishing, LLC
Library of Congress Control Number: 2023900135

ISBN-13: 979-8-9874292-0-4 (hardcover)
ISBN-13: 979-8-9874292-1-1 (paperback)

Peck-A-Long Publishing
14548 Crawford Brook Lane
Delray Beach, FL 33446
peckalongpublishing.com

March 2023
Printed in the United States of America
Illustrations were created digitally.

Publisher's Cataloging-in-Publication data

Names: Thomas, Ruth, 1940-, author. | Thomas, Russell A., 1970-, illustrator.
Title: Tick rex : queen of the woods / by Ruth Thomas; illustrated by Russell A. Thomas
Description: Delray Beach, FL: Peck-A-Long Publishing, LLC, 2023. | Summary: Tick Rex wants to know who is living at the edge of the woods. One summer day, she sets out on an exciting journey.
Identifiers: LCCN: 2023900135 | ISBN: 979-8-9874292-0-4 (hardcover) | 979-8-9874292-1-1 (paperback)
Subjects: LCSH Ticks--Juvenile fiction. | Bullying--Juvenile fiction. | Forest animals--Juvenile fiction. | BISAC JUVENILE FICTION / Animals / Insects, Spiders, etc. | JUVENILE FICTION / Science & Nature / General | JUVENILE FICTION / Social Themes / Bullying
Classification: LCC PZ7.1 .T46 Ti 2023 | DDC [E]--dc23

TICK REX
QUEEN OF THE WOODS

By Ruth Thomas

Illustrated by Russell A. Thomas

**Peck-A-Long
Publishing**
Delray Beach, FL

The animals in the woods named a tiny dark tick, Tick Rex. Why did they give her this name?

The tick did not look like a Tyrannosaurus Rex dinosaur. The tick was tiny. The dinosaur was huge. The wild dinosaur, who lived long ago, liked to bite. The tick liked to bite, too. That is why the animals named her Tick Rex.

"I am Queen of the Woods! Everyone will obey me, or I will bite them and make them sick," said Tick Rex.

Tick Rex lived on the back of a white-tailed deer.
One summer day, Tick Rex wanted to find out who
was living at the edge of the woods.

Tick Rex said,
"White-tailed deer,
take me to the edge
of the woods!"

"No, Tick Rex.
I want to stay here."

"I am Queen Tick Rex," said the little tick. "You must obey me!"

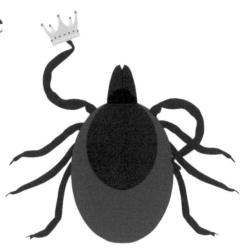

Tick Rex bit the deer on its tail. The deer became **very angry**.

"YOU TICK ME OFF!"

cried the deer.

The deer shook its tail.

Tick Rex fell off the deer.

She landed on a blade of grass.

Soon, a white-footed mouse came by.

"Little tick, who are you waiting for?" asked the mouse.

"I am Queen Tick Rex. Take me to the edge of the woods!"

"Climb onto my back and I will take you there," said the scared mouse.

Tick Rex crawled onto the mouse's back.

The mouse started to run through the woods.

After a while, the mouse became tired and wanted to rest.

"Do not rest now! We will never get to the edge of the woods. You are a lazy mouse," said Tick Rex.

Tick Rex bit the mouse on its tail.
The mouse became **very angry**.

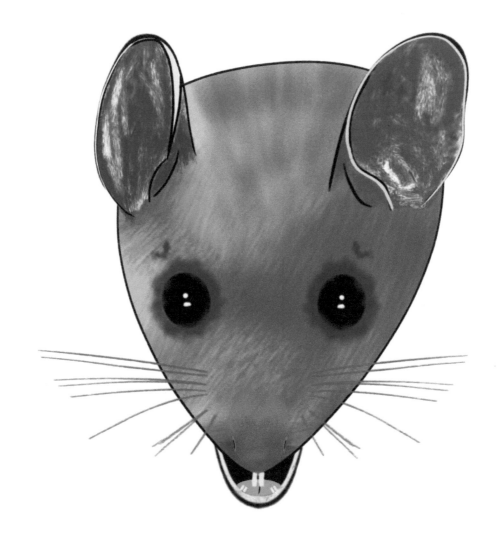

"YOU TICK ME OFF!"

squeaked the mouse.

The mouse flicked its tail and Tick Rex was thrown
to the grassy ground.

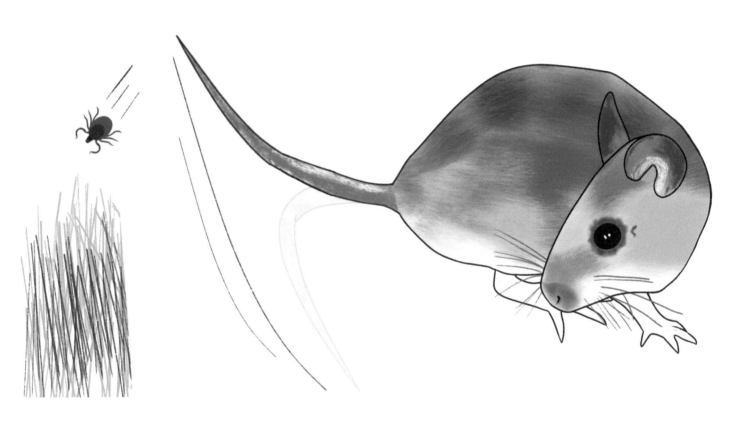

The mouse continued its way,
leaving the tick behind.

"I cannot fly like a bird, but I can crawl. That is what I will do. I will use my eight legs to reach the edge of the woods," said Tick Rex.

Tick Rex began to crawl through the woods when she came upon a raccoon.

"Listen, raccoon! I am Queen Tick Rex. I need you to take me to the edge of the woods."

"Climb onto my tail,"
said the frightened raccoon.

The tick and the raccoon traveled through the woods.

They finally arrived at the edge of the woods and in front of them was a large open field.

"Raccoon, take me through the field," said the tick. "No," said the raccoon, "I do not want to leave the woods."

Tick Rex bit the raccoon on its tail. The raccoon became **very angry**.

"YOU TICK ME OFF!"

snarled the raccoon.

The raccoon wagged its tail dropping Tick Rex to the ground.

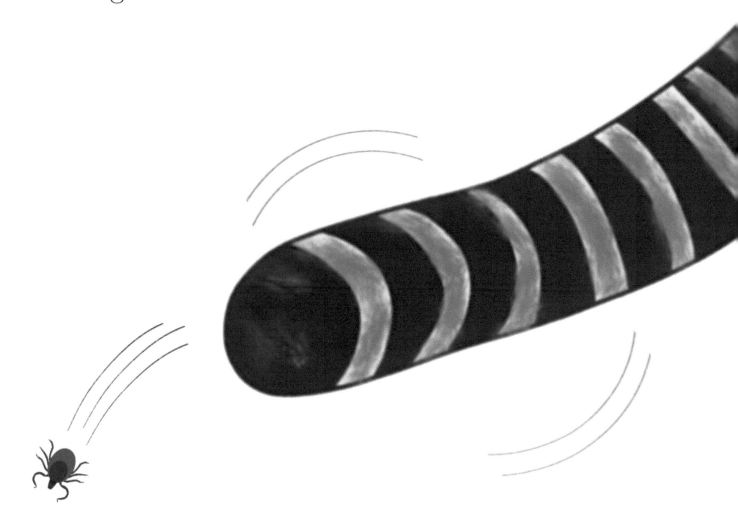

The raccoon ran away.

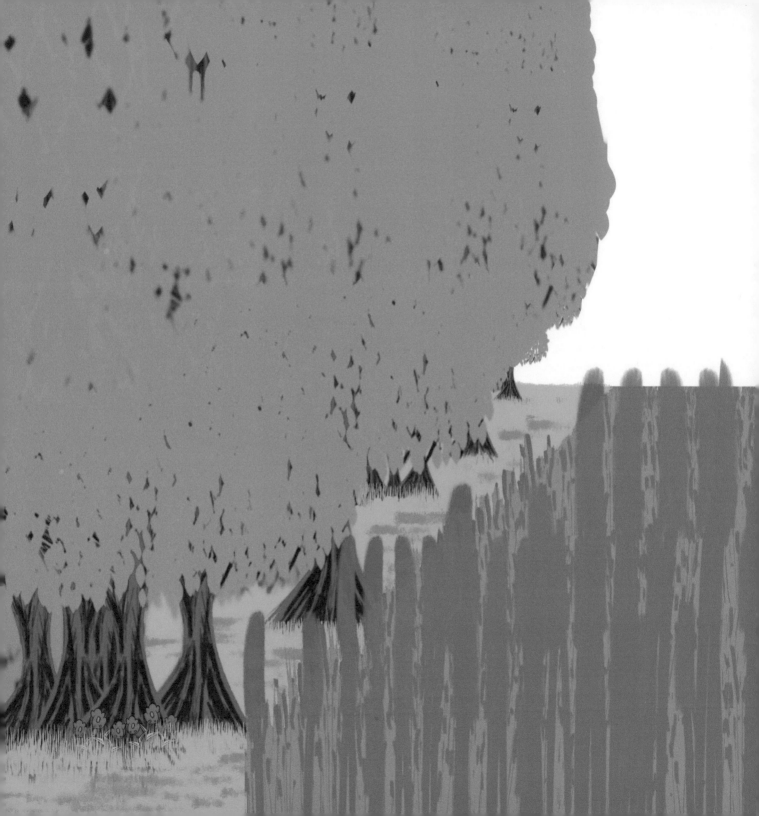

A dog came walking near Tick Rex.

"I am Queen Tick Rex. Take me through the field!"

"Climb onto my tail," said the scared dog.

Nearby was a house. Tick Rex yelled, "Stop here! I want you to take me to that house."

"No," said the dog, "I do not want to go home right now. I just want to keep on running."

Tick Rex bit the dog's tail. The dog became **very angry**.

"YOU TICK ME OFF!"

growled the dog.

The dog wagged its tail.

The tick fell to the ground.

The dog ran away.

Tick Rex crawled to the backyard of the house where two children were doing a puzzle.

The tick climbed up the child's white shirt sleeve.

The mother noticed Tick Rex and yelled, "You are not going to bite my child!"

The mother became **very angry**.

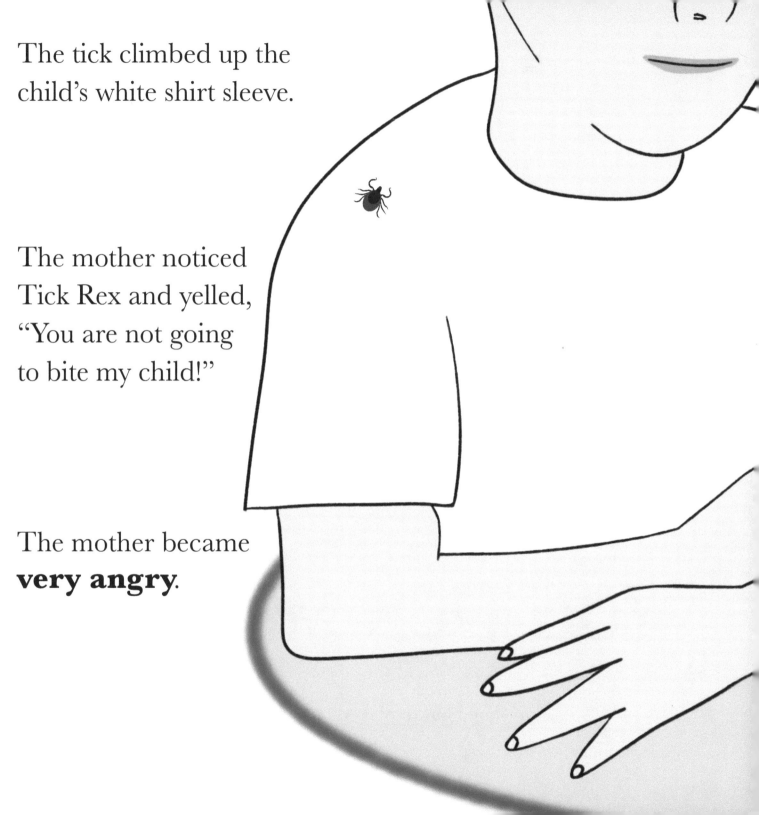

"YOU TICK ME OFF!"

screamed the mother.

The mother flicked the tick off the shirt sleeve.

Tick Rex fell to the ground.

The tick crawled back into the tall grass.
A little while later, a bird landed near Tick Rex.

"I am Queen Tick Rex! I want you to take me back to the woods where the white-tailed deer live."

"I will fly you home," said the frightened bird.

Tick Rex climbed onto the bird's tail. The bird flew into the sky and started flying very fast.

"Stop flying so fast!" said Tick Rex, "I cannot hold on!"

"I like flying fast," said the bird.
Tick Rex bit the bird on its tail.
The bird became **very angry**.

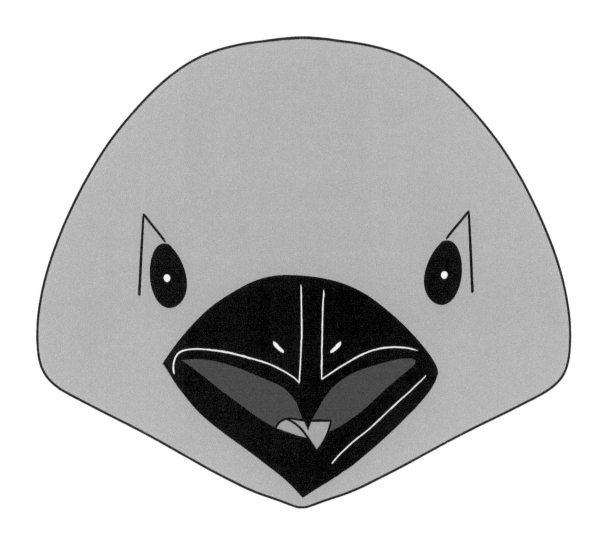

"YOU TICK ME OFF!"

shrieked the bird.

The bird flew even faster through the sky.
Tick Rex could not hold on any longer and fell
off the bird's tail.

The bird returned to the woods and told
all the animals that Tick Rex was gone.

They wondered if Tick Rex would ever return to the woods again.

How a Tick Travels

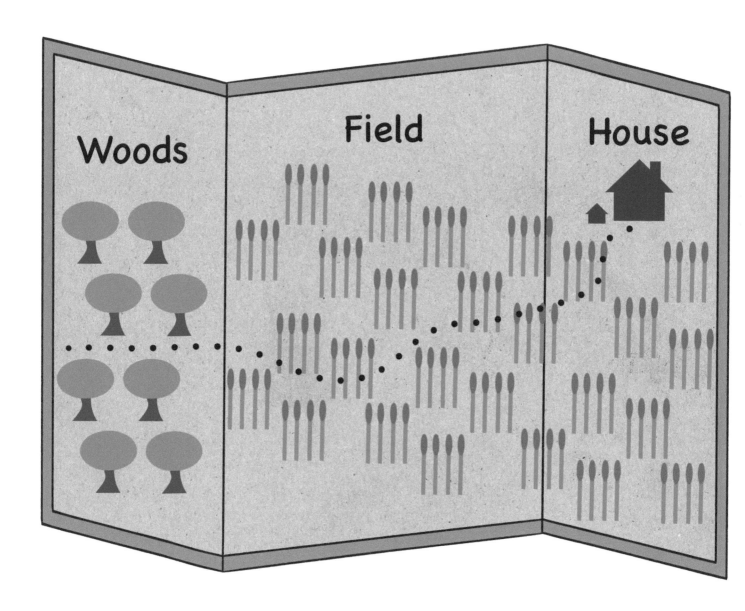

Let Us Review the Story

After reading **Tick Rex: Queen of the Woods**, parents and teachers can ask children to recall several events that happened throughout the story.

1. Who named the tick, Tick Rex?

2. What season did the story take place?

3. How many legs does a tick have?

4. Which animal was lazy?

5. What did Tick Rex do to make all the animals angry?

6. Which animal did Tick Rex travel on in the field?

7. What were the children doing in their backyard?

8. What did the mother see on her child's shirt sleeve?

9. What was the last animal that Tick Rex traveled on?

10. How many tails were in the story?

Bonus Questions

Do you think that the animals liked Tick Rex? Why?

A Message From the Author

Ticks carry Lyme disease. *Tick Rex: Queen of the Woods* makes you become aware of how a tick can travel right up to your doorstep. Their preferred habitats are wooded areas and grasslands. Ticks are spread in the wild by animals like deer, mice, raccoons, and birds. Domestic animals such as dogs can also carry infected ticks. To prevent Lyme disease, parents should check to see that there are no ticks on clothing or pets before entering the house.

— Ruth Thomas

Tick Rex

May is observed as National Lyme Disease Awareness Month

To all the people who have encountered Lyme disease, we hope you will recover and become stronger!

Ruth Thomas

taught preschool for several years after having graduated from Brooklyn College. Her hobbies include painting and writing. She is a proud owner of a large peacock collection. Ruth lives in the sunny state of Florida.

Russell A. Thomas

is an illustrator and presentation design specialist who takes brainstorming thoughts transforming them into unique works of art. He graduated from the University of Central Florida and has certification in digital arts.

Visit us on the Web at www.tickrex.com

CPSIA information can be obtained
at www.ICGtesting.com
Printed in the USA
BVHW012143210523
664619BV00007B/30